MISTER MAGNOLIA

Quentin Blake

LITTLE GREATS

RANDOM CENTURY

LONDON SYDNEY
AUCKLAND JOHANNESBURG

First published in Great Britain 1980
by Jonathan Cape Ltd
First published in *Little Greats* edition 1991
by Random Century Ltd
20 Vauxhall Bridge Road, London SW1V 2SA

Random Century Australia (Pty) Ltd
20 Alfred Street, Milsons Point, Sydney, NSW 2061

Random Century New Zealand Ltd
PO Box 40-086, Glenfield, Auckland 10, New Zealand

Random Century South Africa (Pty) Ltd
PO Box 337, Bergvlei, 2012, South Africa

Printed in Hong Kong
British Library Cataloguing in Publication Data is available

ISBN 1-85681-192-1

Mr Magnolia has only one boot.

He has an old trumpet

that goes rooty-toot —

And two lovely sisters

who play on the flute —

But Mr Magnolia has only one boot.

In his pond live a frog

and a toad and a newt —

He has green parakeets

who pick holes in his suit —

And some very fat owls
who are learning to hoot —
But Mr Magnolia
has only one boot.

He gives rides to his friends

when he goes for a scoot —

And the splash is immense
when he comes down
the chute —

But Mr Magnolia

has only one boot.

Just look at the way that

he juggles with fruit!

The mice all march past
as he takes the salute!

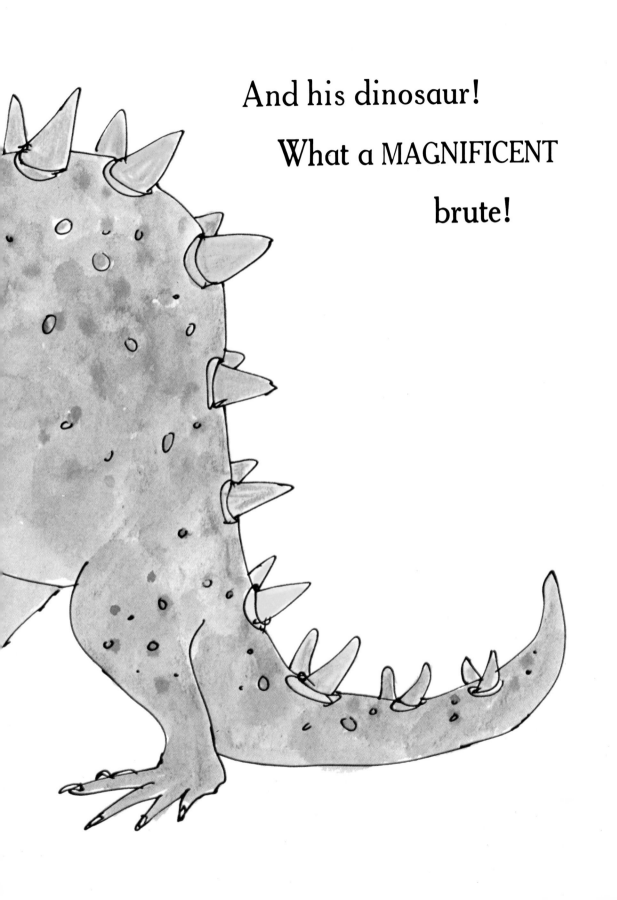

And his dinosaur!

What a MAGNIFICENT

brute!

But Mr Magnolia —

poor Mr Magnolia!

— Mr Magnolia

has

only one boot . . .

Hey —

Wait a minute . . .

Now then . . .

Keep going . . .

What's this?

Look!

It's a boot!

It's a boot!

Whoopee

for Mr Magnolia's

new boot!

Good night.